Janet S. Wong

BUZZ

ILLUSTRATED BY

Margaret Chodos-Irvine

VOYAGER BOOKS • HARCOURT, INC.

Orlando Austin New York San Diego Toronto London

www.harcourt.com

First Voyager Books edition 2002
Voyager Books is a trademark of Harcourt, Inc., registered in the United States of America and/or other jurisdictions.

The Library of Congress has cataloged the hardcover edition as follows:
Wong, Janet S.
Buzz/by Janet S. Wong; illustrated by Margaret Chodos-Irvine.
p. cm.
Summary: As Mommy and Daddy begin their day and get ready for work, a child observes
this morning routine at home as well as the buzzing of a busy bee outside the window.
[1. Morning—Fiction. 2. Bees—Fiction.] I. Chodos-Irvine, Margaret, ill. II. Title.
PZ7.W842115Bu 2000
[E]—dc21   99-6148
ISBN 0-15-201923-5
ISBN 0-15-216323-9

H G F E D C B

The illustrations in this book were created using a variety
of printmaking techniques on Lana printmaking paper.
The display type was created by Margaret Chodos-Irvine.
The text type was set in Syntax Bold.
Color separations by Bright Arts Ltd., Hong Kong
Manufactured by South China Printing Company, Ltd., China
Production supervision by Sandra Grebenar and Wendi Taylor
Designed by Judythe Sieck

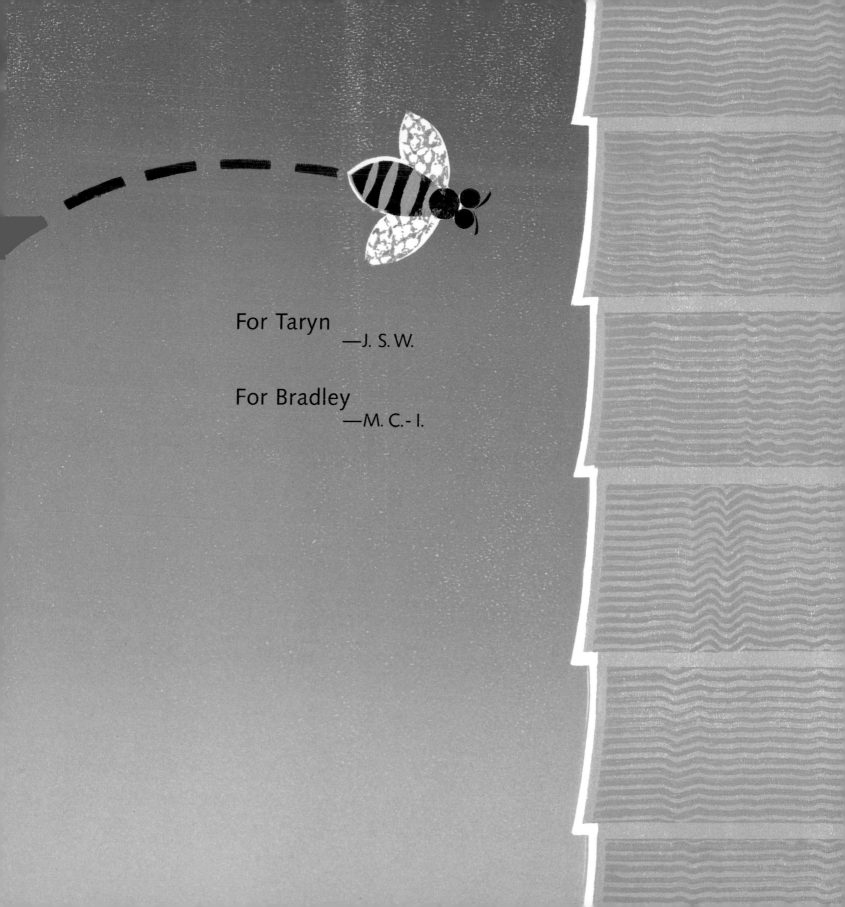

For Taryn
—J. S. W.

For Bradley
—M. C.- I.

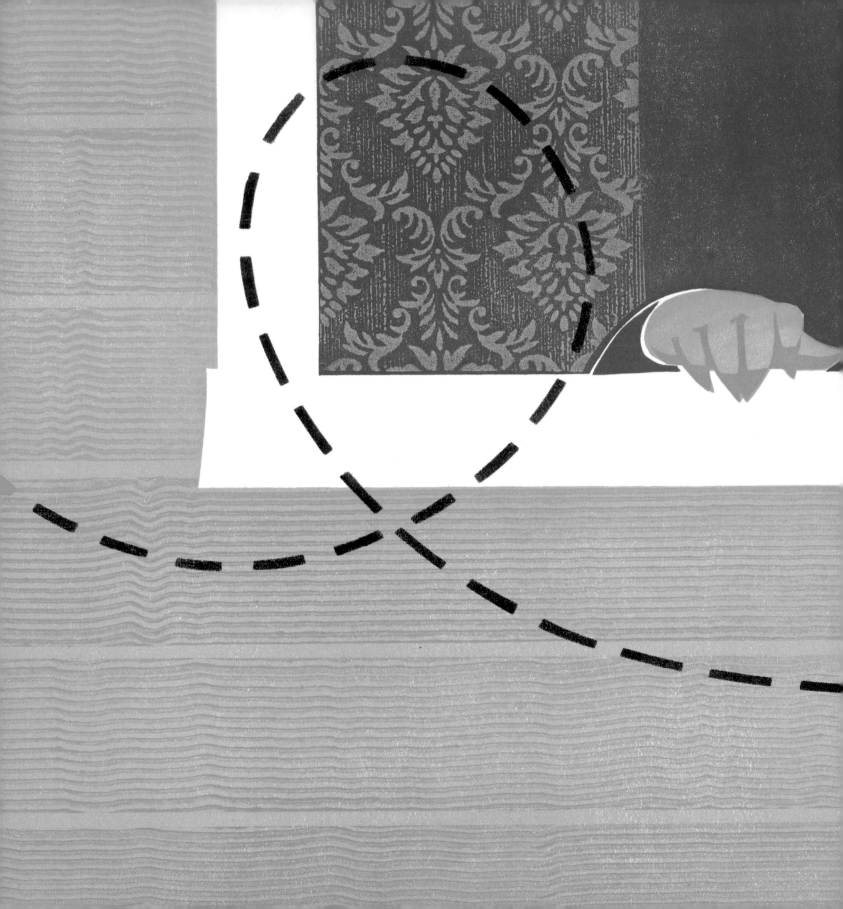

BUZZ

Outside
my window
a bee
eats breakfast
in a big red flower.

BUZZZbuzzzBUZZZbuzzz

Mommy and Daddy snore.

Hooray for the clock!

It's morning!

buzzzBUZZZbuzzzBUZZZ

More snoring

still?

WAKE
UP!

BUZZZZZ

Daddy's silver razor

smooths

his rough face

in one long slow

buzz

and the gardener
mows the grass
across the street.
BUZZZZZZ

I make a banana shake
in the blender
with Mommy
BUZZZZZZZ

and I help Daddy
open the garage door.
BUZZZZZZZZ

I wave good-bye to Daddy
when he leaves for work

and he waves back to me
honking his horn.

BEEP
BEEP!

Mommy grinds coffee
BUZZZZZZZZ

while I fly my airplane
BUZZZZZZZZ

over the oatmeal
BUZZZZZZ

and past the apple juice
BUZZZZZZ—

OH NO!

Splash landing!

And Mommy runs
to catch my cup
  and the apple juice spills

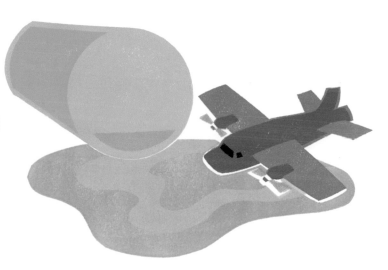

and her toast pops up

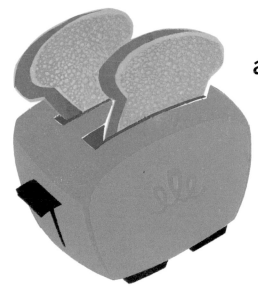

  and the clothes go
  tumbling round
  and round
  and round until—

BUZZZZZ

She runs to the dryer
and drops clothes on the floor

and hops on one leg
to put her right sock on
and hops on her other leg
to put her left sock on

and blows her hair dry
BUZZZZ
until it stands straight up.

BUZZZ

I rush to the
front door when
Grandma comes

and I kiss Grandma
hello

and I kiss Mommy
good-bye

so she can fly

BUZZ outside